Standing Tall in Echoes of Destiny

STANDING TALL IN ECHOES OF DESTINY

Be Blessed !

Poems by

ELMA GABRIEL-MAYERS

Library of Congress Control Number: 2014914969
ISBN: Hardcover   978-1-4990-5373-9
               Softcover   978-1-4990-5374-6
               eBook   978-1-4990-5375-3

Rev. date: 09/19/2014

To order additional copies of this book, contact:
Xlibris LLC
1-888-795-4274
www.Xlibris.com
Orders@Xlibris.com
657853

CONTENTS

Dedication

First, I must thank God for the inner strength, which lend aid to my writing inspiration, and for the endurances to assure me that the reality of oneness is not about being alone, but for the purpose of finding one's self and recognizing that person within you, a precious soul to tap in to every moment, minute, or second, one day at a time.

To my very special friend Rev. Dr. Chester Searles, may God continue to bless him and Janice, providing them the blessings that are required for them to continue their service in this world, to Audrey Kydd-Lewis and Fred Prescod for their undivided, genuine reinforcement.

To my dear son KP for being a blessing, for understanding our many ups and downs, knowing that the green grass can at times turn brown, that the world will always be beautiful-all depends on the eyes of the beholder. To my many relatives, friends and community associates you are surely not the least but the main contributors which propel the content of this book.

In every project there are many persons who helped in making this possible, it is impossible to list all their names; however, I thank everyone who contributed to this project.

Introduction

Elma's first experience of poetry writing was during her high school years in the mid-sixties; however, even though literature and sketching was her most-liked subject, due to limited encouragement and fear of critique, she failed to pursue what in the last twenty years became apparent. Her yearning passion to express her inner thoughts ballooned not only in writing but also in verbal expression, a once extremely shy young woman who seemed to prioritize her time to the benefit of seniors and children, extending compassion where ever. Born on the island of Saint Vincent and the Grenadines in the eastern Caribbean and having migrated to Canada in the sixties, acquired the label of a community activist for her stance on social and other community issues; being endorsed for her integrity by persons of all culture, religion, race or creed. This is her first book of a collection of poems of the last ten years. She is a promising self-motivated author.

Be Inspired / Inspiration

Challenging each day knowing that tomorrow will come whether you are here or not is a great approach of combat. See the beauty and all the possibilities, look at the operation of the hour glass, it flows so evenly and so quietly; in patience another hour goes, and then it balances over to continue the next. No stress, no cares, it flows. So is this world meant to be a beautiful people as each one can see, as the air you breathe it is for you and for me. It is ours, it is free; don't take for granted the generosity. Your happiness is in your hand.

Move On! Move On!

The morning appears dazzling with gold
One never knows what the day will unfold—
But off you go with the chores of the day
Hoping to fulfill those goals of yesterday

Before my eyes the day glides away;
While loved ones prepare for the end of the day—
Expectations of greetings and goodies for sharing,
To adorn the closing of a weary day;

The golden sun dims over the hazy horizon,
A silent goodbye to the world on this way,
The sea reflects a thankful glaze—
As the clouds gives its vision to the fortunate gaze.

Move on! Move on! Oh, you fortunate few—
You are anointed with the tranquility of peace as a glow.
Move on! Move on! You are not alone,
The peace within will reign on in atone.

(Writing inspired through a photo shot of a setting of the sun in the Caribbean).

Experience Epiphany

As we experience life's destiny,
Demands are great as we all can see,
It matters not what the burden be;
Let's stride on with "transparency.

The years past were meant to be,
So now it's time to master the theory.
From our mistakes we now can see,
The focus really should be on unanimity.

As a people from this tribe
So unique on this our land so blessed;
Fate cannot deny a torch we must together hold—
Re-affirms; envision amid one hope.

Let's look at what the odds could be,
As development is part of our destiny,
With hearts and soul, as patriots let's uphold
The Constitution as our founders has told.

Our goal is to augment their dreams of old,
Enlightening their off-springs of the untold;
The years that past and those to come,
It is our responsibility to share with some.

So as we move on in harmony,
Let's pitch out all animosity;
With love and trust; respect for humanity—
And with dignity, we are sure to experience epiphany.

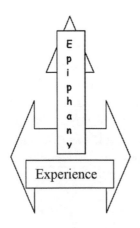

The Mind

The mind-it holds the master plan.
It guides you; hope you understand,
The risk of life is in your hand—
The choice is yours, so take your stand.

Don't wait for one to make your plan,
The torch, you see, it's in your hand
He promised to help as you go along—
If only you can understand.

The light shines bright for you to see,
What he has already set out for thee.
I hope one day you'll soon see,
The special qualities within me.

I have to go on with my plan,
'Cause you don't seem to understand.
My mind-it holds the master plan,
One day, I know, you'll be my fan.

And as you move on with your plan,
I hope one day you'll understand,
That love is more than just a fad—
Your happiness is in your hand.

The Journey of Life

The puzzle of life's reality
Will sometimes bring uncertainty,
Your dreams at times
Are blossoms of the imaginary truth—
The after mat confusion of a seemly realm of life
That might surface on your journey
When you least expect.

You waver in the distance
As your world seem to sleep,
Now your comfort zone is at risk
As you float upon your feet,
The shivers are for real
As you look beyond your dreams,
Should I be sure and take a chance—
On what it seem to be?

Or should I let my prison cell—
Take full control of me?
The confusion of my inner self
Has captivated my soul,
And my spiritual connections
Have overwhelmed my self-control,
Be careful what you wish for, as I was always told.
The Joys of life could come around as many dreams unfold,
Your inner strength will make you sound
And purify your soul.
Upon the tide you float along, with confident you hold!
The time has come, don't circumvent.
Enjoy your days of old.

Unification

Where has it gone, our purity?
And let's not forget the generosity.
Where has it gone, our empathy?
So let's not trample on our society.

Where has it gone, our integrity?
We people of morality.
Where has gone, that spirituality?
That was there since before liberality.

Where has it gone, our loyalty?
It is critical to building unity.
Where has it gone, our continuality?
That led to finality.

Where has it gone, our simplicity?
That helps in humility.
Where has it gone, our creativity?
It is part of our heredity.

Where has it gone, our rituality?
That creates our humanity.
Please! Let's strengthen our nationality,
And stride on for unanimity.

Being one's self brings much peace to one's life, a sense of gratification that generates so freely the vital sustenance to good health, aid by such humility. Exhibiting much tranquil accolade to one's demure.

—Elma Gabriel June 24, 2014

Let the Trinity Reign

Oh people of Christianity,
Why invest on wasted energy?
He promised to give you security,
If you're focused on the Trinity.

He knows your hearts since at the start;
Your blueprints were endorsed as he died on the Cross.
On the lot of your church, let's clear the curse,
Then in Jesus' name, through his blood, you will gain.

Your struggles are in vain if he does not reign.
With unity and love you will get your fame.
All talents and gifts are in his name,
And success is waiting behind that shade.

Your jealousies and envies defeats your growth,
And the spirit grieves as it is in besieged.
So lighten up your hearts as it was at the start,
And let freedom reign so his spirit will bring gain.

It is imperative that the church is sound,
For a healthy body, we must work with love.
At the end of our road, heaven will be our home,
So for Jesus' sake, let the Trinity reign.

The Air Restrained by His Destiny

Our goal of life, it may seem as our choice,
Like the air we breathe, it is there for our needs;
It is ours; it's free; it is for you and for me—
And we take for granted his generosity.

So we do as we please and are sure to succeed.
"Wow! I can see, I can hear, and my phone lines are clear.
I can reach through the world and can speak loud and clear.
For sure there is air, and my friends, they can hear.

"As I hail to the east, west, to the north and the south,
It is real and a tool, and it is real cool,
No ink, no trail, no one to curtail,
Our tongues are ours, and it carries the tattle tales.

"As we lurk our plans, then in confidence we'll stand.
With all their support, our strategies we'll withhold.
The power is ours, and we are sure of their trust.
It is great and a joy to be placed at the top."

But let's not take for granted his generosity,
And remember, our success —it all depends on him.
As we work for love and for charity,
Our integrity in time is restrained by his destiny.

Holy Clouds

Glory! Glory! They are so holy—
Watch the clouds; they seem so lonely,
They move around as snails that are weary—
And wait for light to make them cheery.

Holy! Holy! They come with glory—
So we can see and be more surely,
To reach the height and think of glory—
As we experience the zest that makes us holy.

The Trampling Ground

The world is a trampling ground.
Just look as the horses run.
In confidence they trot, with focused eyes,
Head gently tilted—aimed for the top.

The world is a trampling ground.
As the beast move round and round,
With minds alert, they secure their turf,
On this great place, our planet earth.

On this trampling ground that we call earth,
It is our means as a place of birth.
As generation goes, and the new one comes,
We take for granted the sinking sand.

This morning you awoke, and you felt grand.
The earth, it's yours to trample on.
So you forgot to thank that great one,
Who provided you with this great birth land!

So go on trampling on this our land.
It is yours and mine to do what we can,
But don't forget to take that stand.
The goal is to be at his right hand.

So as you trample on this land,
Remember where this earth came from.
That day of rapture is sure to come—so prepare—
For that flight promises to be the best one!

Emotions

Is love a fiction, and if there is love, have you found your own description for it? Should it be lasting, one sided, imbalanced, connected to material values, imaginary? So then; how is it related to emotions? And if such emotion tells me that I love and it is "love," so why wouldn't the other connect the same message? What a confusion, when what should be a personal feeling is at times controlled by the opinion of friends, relatives, your integrity and standards, but should love be controlled in time through destiny? Love can only survive of untainted emotion, a beauty that pours from within, not by material attraction or attachment. It says to come as you are, tried and true, the embracing of me and you, of two persons so pure, so real. "Yours are for me as mine is for you". And so it will last as two hearts encompasses at the same time, same space; even apart, your thoughts connect as no one can separate such emotional mesh.

The Beauty Within

Can you feel the serenity, a peace deep down within?
Come, experience the touch, the energy—it is much!
It is connected to a heart always ready to fulfill its part,
Like a soaring eagle so beautiful and so smart.

Can you feel the energy of the beauty that lies within?
So large, so refreshing, full of warmth to make you calm,
So true and sincere, ends your doubts and draws near.
Let go . . . come feel the touch—the energy is much.

Can you feel the touch by that beauty within?
It is catching and revealing to those even in sin.
It is forgiving and cleansing and dispels through the skin,
A glow that stays forever, radiance from within!

Can you see the glow experienced from the beauty
within?
It is permanent, it is a splendor, and it excels from within,
So gorgeous as is seen, a mystique it would seem.
To the eyes it is far and few in between.

Bewildered by such charm but refreshed from within.
A touch of that energy has cleansed us of our sins.
The peace and serenity you can feel deep within.
As an eagle, you soar—it's the beauty within!

Nobody Knows

Nobody knows the joy I feel
Within my heart—it's clear and clean.
Nobody knows what's on the scene,
Because our life is just a dream.

Nobody sees what I have seen.
My eyes are clear and full of gleam.
Nobody knows where I am going,
Because no one knows where I have been.

Nobody knows the love I feel,
As no one knows that it is real.
Nobody knows the time to kneel,
For some sentiments are so unreal.

Nobody knows when it's that time.
No! No one else but him on high.
Nobody saves you when he calls,
So let us share the joy after all.

I'll come

Life wasn't fun, so I thought I'll come,
To visit the corner church with some,
I got around and shared the songs,
And thought I'll come back for the next round.

It feels so good when Sunday comes,
Because I know that the church is sound.
The hymns, they sing with such a swing—
That makes me want to move all things.

The church, they are so warm and cheery-
They make me feel that I should share.
The Pastors, they are so full of cheer.
I now know where they find their flare.

The joy I feel when I'm there,
Makes me feel that I am near,
To him who died to make us shine,
So let's be prepared in the meantime.

A Fool's Green

It looked green as it would seem,
An immaculate view my eyes have seen.
A simple life, it would appear.
How nice it will be to be there.

So opportunity I seek
To meet with you at a retreat.
I planned and looked for just that time . . .
For you and me to see eye to eye.

It took some time, I must agree,
To catch your eyes in unity.
With faith and patience, I insisted,
That someday soon we'll reminisce.

The time came, and our eyes connected.
Is this for real, or just a fake?
The joy within brought such relief.
I didn't care for those in grief.

As time went by and the green turned brown,
The immaculate scene became a dream.
And as I looked back where I've been,
The green, I know, was only a fool's dream.

And now my eyes have seen the light.
I have to bear the grit of plight,
And hope that those I put to grief,
Would work with me and be relieved.

A Special Day

You are special as I can see,
My love for you will always be,
So stay as handsome as can be,
Your happiness means a lot to me.

This day was made so we can be—
In truth, one love, two souls on a spree,
But it's difficult as I can see,
So go ahead as love sets you free.

My Heart, My Cares

My heart, it leaps and then it sleeps.
I smile because I am sanctified.
The joy I feel is what you would dream.
My spirit, it never felt so serene.

The worries of life have passed me by.
The joys within, it makes me sing.
My spirit is now re-energized,
And the plight of life was once upon a time.

I pray that you will understand,
That life is just a passing pang.
The light must be your focused plan—
It guides you straight to his right hand.

I pray that you will understand,
Deserting you is not my plan.
The breath of life is his sanction,
And the choice is his, so I go along.

My soul is at rest, and he knows best.
He assured me that he will take care of the rest.
My family, he said, they are blessed.
Please understand as you withstand the test.

No fear, no snare, I'll be always near.
He promised me he will let me take care.
I sit right next to his right hand.
He is a man who carries through with his plan.

I am at peace and will now sleep.
Thanks for your love—it is so deep.
Your time, your cares, your heart full of cheers,
So-long, my dears; remember the Lord cares.

Family

We all do have families, being those of whom we were born through or by adoption—they are all family, those who should be near and dear to our hearts, the security-blanket concept, that which we were or must have been wrapped in following the exit from our mothers' wombs into this world. A place where some may, at that critical moment, call birth, having been thrown into an immediate state of individuality, helpless but protected by a redeemer who compasses the emotions of the family organism. The mystic sentiment of the family circle, which still takes preference over friends, as friends may come and friends may go, but the family traits have no place to go.

The Family Show

The family is the tree of life,
It bears its fruit and shades its plight.
We are all children of that sight,
So let's learn to fly the kite.

And even when it seems to drop,
Don't stop! 'Cause it will come right back.
And when it starts to fly again,
Watch out! And try to win the game.

Though friends may come and friends may go,
The family stays even when it's low.
Our life is just a picture show,
So let us all stay in a row.

And as you catch up with good friends,
Remember, this is just a bend.
The family's ship will sail at end,
When Noah's Ark is ready then!

So let us all pray for the wind,
'Cause time passes as the tree swings.
The air we breathe will cleanse our soul,
And with good courage, we can be made whole.

Marriage Is a Partnership

Marriage is a partnership
Where spirits unite,
A love that quenches the hollow thirst
And lends the soul a true escort.

Marriage is a partnership
That sometimes seems a chore,
But when in unity it's done,
The effort seems as none.

Marriage is a partnership
Where two are bound with trust,
Of love and faith that help you grow
And brave the world with grace.

Marriage is a partnership
That pleases the family's face,
And when the offspring comes along
A joy spreads in the place.

Marriage is a partnership
That demands a little space,
So each can share and understand
The nucleus of love and charms!

Marriage is a partnership
Formed through the grace of God,
So with his command you take an oath
That binds the heart and soul.

So on this date, forever it will be told.
See, your commitment is depicted on that scroll.
We pray for joy; we pray for love
And showers of blessings from the heavens above.

The Baby Comes

The joy shines within your face,
In expectancy to fill your space,
And as he comes into this place,
We know he will share your love and grace.

So as he laughs and jumps around,
We will pass by to share some fun,
With you, the dad, and that dear son,
God bless him as his birthday comes.

The Trait of a Father

Father, you are the foundation of our being,
The framework that supports our flesh,
The fountain of the waters,
The fragrance of the flowers of our surroundings,
The fruits of the gardens,
You are our friends,
The fighters at the front line
The foreigner in our land,
You are the leader of the flocks,
The fosterer to our success,
The fiction of our life,
The fundamentals to our belief,
The funnel to our faithfulness,
You are the mediator to our fury,
The fuse to our vision,
The footstool to our strength,
The fund for our fares,
The freeway to our freedom,
The furrow to our future,
Furthermore, you are the fun at the fair,
And foremost in our life—
You are the floodlight to our dreams.

I Love You, Mommy

The child, she is so full of grace,
As the sun shines in her face.
She is happy as you can see—
She smiles and says, "I love you, Mommy!

So dry your tears and remember Christ—
He died to save you and me.
I am in heaven as you once told me.
My wings, they fit for eternity.

I see my friends and family,
And they are happy that he saved me.
He promised that one day you'll see,
That heaven is secure and free.

So share your love and spread his words,
And tell the world that he is Lord,
You are special as he agrees,
That's why you are my mommy."

The Trinity of Our Feeling Father's Love!

Our Father is a man of feelings,
His heart emits the most cordial mind,
Of radiance and amity,
As pinnacles of blessings pouring down from above.

Our Father expresses unmatchable love,
Flexibility in forgiving, promise through atonement from above,
Of the Trinity in one Godhead, a father,
One person with three natures but in one spirit of love.

He implies no restriction,
But the free will of choices allotted to all,
As his blessings are forever,
Conferred to the obedience of the calling in our lives.

So let's not take for granted,
That deemed freedom as we live.
He is meant to be more than just a father here to give.
He is a positive example, the blueprint of the life we ought to live!

Hence, as we trod on daily,
Let's refrain from being the judge,
As to what and who is holy.
'Tis his duty, the trait, our Father's job,
With such promise of serenity, guided by such a feeling Father's love.

And while our mission is for glory,
Showered by his compassionate love,
Via our works, choices, gratitude, and sorrows,
Devoted we'll stand by the Trinity of our feeling Father's love!

The Wailing Mother

She wails from deep down within her soul,
No visible tears you will ever behold,
As her inner self infuses and restores,
Like a generator refresher to such weary soul.

The wailing mother, she smiles and also plays,
As for her children, her strength she must display,
She must go on no matter if the world turns gray,
Her wailing soul remains invisible to this day.

Life

Let's not assume that life is a stone's throw for anyone, as we were all born on the same world—yes, at various times, locations, culture, nationalism, color, class, and creed—thereby poses what we soon realize an automatic struggle as individuals so different but beautiful and so unique. As life goes on, we're supposed to mature but soon become more confused as to the real meaning of maturity.

Life, for some reason or another, seems to have become more complex, and at times one may ask, where is this freedom? Am I not supposed to be free? These are the most dangerous of questions; be careful where the answer can lead you!

Believe it or not, but you were always in control of you. The problem is that due to fear, you may have failed to grab that freedom at such critical point. Here is where your principles may have aided the way you choose to go—may it be religion, culture, radicalism, standards, the will, society, or whatever it may be. Mark my word, it is very real and it plays a major part in what I call life's dash.

Today

The day looks bleak
Through the fog we seek—
To find what's there
And fight defeat.

The joy we feel
We know not why—
'Cause life seems like
It is a lie.

He gave me faith
For forty times—
And said that I
Must not stop trying.

He is so sweet
A real treat—
To seek his face
In such retreat.

The ups and downs
Of life we found—
But the dear Lord
He stays around.

So stand your ground
As he is sound—
No matter what
Just hold on strong.

The Storm Proceeds

Oh, Great and Mighty One, we ask your mercy grant.
Anoint us, Lord, your grace we seek, your blessings we receive.
Our flesh is weak; the hurts are deep, but yours alone we breathe.
The joy of life we think we need, without your love proceed.
Oh Lord! We cry but shed no tear; the eyes we see deceit.
The air we breathe is choked with dust,
And in our hearts the storm proceeds.
We run and run to find your love, and no one knows the creed.
Oh Lord! Have mercy, grant us peace.
Your blessing we'll receive.
When we proceed with faith and trust in you, our Father's creed,
We will succeed and share the joy and breathe your air of peace.
Oh God! We come to you with hope; deliverance we request.
In you we will forever seek eternal joy of peace.
With you we know that all will be well when we find eternity.

Freedom

They who resist the perils of control will not be intimidated by the threat of fear but will shine in life's freedom, viewing any stumbling block as an opportunity to develop their vision and exercise their creativity.

—Elma Gabriel June 18, 2014

Life Is a Risk

Life is hard to understand,
The world, it seems to be full of sand,
And when the breeze blows where we stand,
We spin within whirling sand.

We walk in a daze upon the sand,
And seem to sink where we stand,
Our strength, sometimes it is not grand,
But our life, we try to understand.

Life is a risk, so let's hold hands,
'Cause all of us are in that sand,
With strength we'll fight with all our might,
To defeat that whirlwind as it strikes.

In Times Like These

It is so very sad to hear,
And I know it is your pain to bear.
But be assured that I am near,
With you and yours, I shed some tears.

This'd hard for you, as it's a mother's dread,
To lose a child so near and dear.
As from the womb we feel a tear,
A broken heart, a woman's fear.

What can one say in times like these?
No word seems enough to ease the freeze.
But to you and yours, I send my love,
Just as it came down from above.

I pray that God will soothe your pain,
Like raindrops that fall upon the pane.
As you look beyond the distant fields,
For the miseries of life's unspoken dreams.

And as the whistling sound of the morning planes,
Fades like a dream yet once have been.
Such are the pains of life's despair,
As we connect through distant air.

So look beyond what the eyes can see,
And remember that life is just really a dream—
A vacation as was appointed to be,
As eternity is our destiny.

So there he is, up in the skies,
Shouting the song "In the sweet Bye-and-Bye"
In God's right hand, he takes his stance,
Right next to him is our family's clan!

Dedicated in memory of Rohan V. C. Ryan
July 25, 1975 — April 23, 2014

Mentors

Who are these people? How are they selected? And who selects them for you? The fact remains that they are your choice, chosen based on your expectation or something like that, possibly stemming from your nurturing stage. The principle taught to you by way of your parents and guardians could be from that which was deemed to have been considered as the expected behavioral epic of their time. So you seem to have stuck there even though political strategies, many changes have taken place, the epidemic to generational gaps, the conflict to our chaos, and the nightmare to stagnation within our generations.

But as an individual, you will continue to choose a mentor. It is part of your insecurities, and you will also be genuinely proud of him or her. Just do not be disappointed if your mentor seems to have detoured as was assessed. Don't, as your mentor is an individual, and so are you! I will always love my mentors as I believe that their good have overpowered their weaknesses.

"It Is Well with My Soul," She Whispered to Us All

A first lady as she was born to be,
With much poise and stature, her demure reveals,
So generous and caring, always geared up for sharing,
Oh, what exquisite a person was she.

A land of independence was the main intent,
Her sweetheart, a hero, so courageous and free,
So devoted was she, so loyal and true,
So inspiring, a mentor, a friend, a sister, an aunt.

A perfect life she never assumed,
In a world that is known to be full of gloom,
As a woman of strength, she faced day by day,
Her role, she knew just how well to play.

Our leading lady, she made us proud,
In our history the first hero's woman was she,
Now on balanced wings she moves joyfully through the skies,
As she anticipates for the past few years after his good-bye.

So let's dry all our tears as we celebrate her life,
The great reunion of our loved ones in the sky,
As the trumpets sound and she answered the call,
"It is well with my soul," she whispered to us all!

That Smile!

As her heavenly smile spreads on her face,
Those pearly-white teeth so-erectly placed,
One can feel the warmth of her true embrace,
As she thanks God for all his grace.

Her eyes, they speak a silent word,
One does not wander within her world.
"Girl, come for your hug"—as she would shout—
"Today is the day we've all heard about."

Overwhelmed by her love as she whispers the word,
"God loves you, girl, hold faith, just hang on.
Heaven is nearer than we may have thought—
It is all about love as we have been taught."

As she holds my hand and the praises start,
I can hear the word flows straight from her heart,
"God, I love you so and for all that you've started.
I can feel your grace deep down in my heart."

"You are here, I know, 'cause I can see the glow.
The reflection of your light has stolen the show.
Rejoice, oh people, and unite in one row.
This'd a blessing to be part of this picture show."

Her warmth, her cheers, has overcome her smears.
Her approach to life was without fear.
Her burden was carried in Christ's care.
She is a beacon, a mentor, as she leaves here.

Oh, how fortunate we are to be touched by her hands.
Let's rejoice and be glad to have been her fan.
Let's sing for joy and clap our hands,
For it is her request that we be as grand.

As she shakes her tambourine with heart full of pride,
And her teeth glitter between those gorgeous smiles,
She says, "So long, my dears, it's the end of my mile.
I am glad you are happy, so now I will take my flight!"

Let's Recompense

Those were the days, so let's reflect!
She was a symbol of confidence.
She went on her way as though to say,
"I know I am great, you'll realize that someday."

As she strode the hall with grace and poise,
"Be quiet! I say, boys and girls.
It's time for class, hence shut your mouths!
Be quiet! Or I will send you out."

Her hair jet-black, we wished for her locks.
They bounce along when she would trot.
We stood in attention, in respect,
And tipped on our toes as we mocked her steps.

To misjudge her was a fatal error.
In the principal's office, Timmie gave no favor.
That strap we knew was hard and sound.
Being in that office was really no fun.

Once in a while she will give us a smile,
Assuring us that our teacher could be pleasant and mild.
Her dimples so deep, to see them was our treat.
We will miss her when she goes into retreat.

We'll make her talk because she was so smart,
That's why she was the head of the staff.
Without her, we knew the fun will not last,
That's why at Intermediate High…she was the boss.

Today her heels are still high,
And her eyes still glow as her words confidently flow.
We love you, Miss, more than you'll ever know.
You are the mentor, the flame to our torch.

Ladies on the Go!

You Ladies on the Go, why are you so?
Where do you go when things are low?
You seem to care but disappear,
And leave a sister to go to tear.

You share your joys and discuss your foes,
As you journey to work with your dreams all thrown,
And no one really knows how far you got to go,
As you embrace that journey on the Go.

Your promise is to support and be true on your report,
As you travel on the Go, unaware, but too far to go.
Some days you hope that the sisters will support,
And be true in their report—because it seems so far to go.

You carry your luggage and bundle your cares,
Good-bye, as you prepare to descend the stairs.
Your day, you pray, will end a good way,
So you can share the joys and prepare for the next day.

In sincerity! To all the ladies I travelled to work with on the Go-Train.

Nationalism

We are all nationals of some place somewhere on this planet. What is really important is our obligation and patriotism, the depth of our commitment and to which country our patriotism lies. Some of us, through immigration, have dedicated our lives to an adoptive country, but deep down within our soul, we seem to have an irresistible love-commitment to the country of our birth. The most mystic sensation as a people is that our soul, as we age, seems to become more connected to those earlier years of that dash through life, thereby lending sacrifice to our adoptive country through our doctrine of gratefulness versus ungratefulness. However, one should not feel any sort of guilt because of their deep and compassionate love for his or her birth land, as it is an uncontrollable experience, a maternal connection that allows the freedom to embrace those occasions to be devoted, to commune, to share, and to take a stance. Being a loyalist adds value to one's esteem, which can only be experienced during the struggles on such journey, the declaration to your nationalism.

Hand in Hand

Hand in hand, let's build our land,
The grace of God, his mercy stands.
That we will share in unity,
And spread the joy of prosperity.

Our foreparents' pain and sweat we bear,
Because we have not learned to care.
We ask that you will grant us ear,
So we can hear and learn to share.

Give us the light, oh God, we pray,
That we can see more every day.
Our leaders' mission we perceive,
And work with vision to achieve.

Oh God, we know that you will grant,
The vision of our parent plan.
To be as one and one in all,
And build our nation hand in hand.

Come In on the Tea Hatter Party

Yes, they wondered whether I'll come,
To join in on the tea hatter fun.
But if they knew me and the real person I am,
They will know that I will not miss this one.

So you see, I am here to join in on the fun,
And to tell you where I really came from.
So open your ears for my introduction,
And inhale the aroma of my sanction.

I am a Vinci from the Vinci Land,
So that makes me Saint Vincentian.
I appear airy, but it is part of my clan,
Breadfruit and codfish are what I'd grown on.

I enjoyed the fresh air from the sea and hills,
And now in this country, the forced air is what kills.
So today I am launching an alternate plan,
That is sure to enhance your and my life span.

My business is air import via the CARICOM land,
It is the alternative to smelling grand.
Your hats will be made of herbs from my land,
And a commission will be given to you and your pal.

So now that you are part of my business plan,
You have no choice but to be my fan.
Come, inhale my tea hatter air,
And your special orders, I look forward to be had.

I am the expert of the tea hatter plan,
Circulating fresh air straight from Vinci Land.
So here I am, as airy as can be,
Flashing the air freshener at this tea hatter party.

The Caribbean, a Place

In the Caribbean is a place to be,
The love of God, it shines on thee.
The goal is to bring unity,
And bless the islands of the Caribbean.

The natives there, they are the best,
With hearts that make you feel at rest.
They come from all across the globe,
With lots of hope and love and dreams.

They wandered there, unaware,
Their iniquities, we know will disappear.
That God will grant them time to share,
And plant a seed so it can bear.

The islands are treasured in hearts full of cheers,
Of endurance that makes one cry a tear.
The joy it brings makes all sing,
Forever let all praise the King.

This is our home; we welcome you here!
To enjoy our beaches and all that you crave.
That God will grant us all that's dear,
And bless us all as we flourish here.

Oh Blessed Land of This Heritage, We Come

This land, so beautiful and free,
How could we not commit to thee?
We are children of your dynasty,
So a part of you we'll always be.

We are who we are because of you,
The essence of your love so true,
And from your hills the sky's so blue,
Countless blessings are shimmering down on you.

Our valleys beam as the water streams,
The gardens green to enhance the scene.
Is this a dream, as it would seem?
Or is this paradise, a territorial delight?

Skyscrapers we see as they grazed our skies,
Into the horizon as we wave them good-bye.
They are there, and we are here,
But in our hearts we know they are near.

Oh, lands as one! As a people we come,
To lift you up and make you sound.
We stand firm, without a frown,
Oh blessed land of our heritage, we come.

CARICOM Torch Run

They cried, they jumped, they cheered, and they laughed.
Sometimes it seemed the hope was lost.
But on their knees they felt at ease.
The treaty of Chaguaramas will move with breeze.

Let's carry the torch, for the time has come,
To unite in the name of CARICOM.
So as we move from town to town,
The Caribbean will be one territorial ground.

Colonialism will remain with some,
As the CARICOM torch runs from land to land.
In silence we'll jointly take our stand,
To support that chapter our heroes planned.

"Together now"—that is what it means,
A single market in the Caribbean.
The united symbol, a territorial dream,
The Treaty of Chaguaramas is now for real.

Let's cry, let's jump, let's cheer, and let's laugh.
Let's join and celebrate an accomplished past.
With strength to strength we support the land,
And move forward with our mandated plan.

Build Your Country, Support Local Industry

Our industry, we hope that it will be
Recognized by you and me,
And by your generosity,
Our country can be strong and free.

With gifted hands, we craft our thoughts
And write with love upon the charts.
We ask that you will look across
And support this country with its task.

Our produce strives on natural soil,
Our local laborers toil and toil.
As children of this fertile soil,
We count on you as we toil.

Your health is what we focus on,
So make sure that you understand.
Your gifts and thoughts are in the sand,
That bore the fruit that's in this can.

So let us count on your support,
To build this country as we go forth.
No matter where on earth you rest,
This country's produce is the best.

Reality

Reality is the understanding of what's real, and by doing so, one becomes more well-disposed to the daily episodes of life. You become a realist, a stronger person not for yourself but as a supporter to those around you, helping one to overcome selfishness as you can more clearly see that side, this side, and the other side. Being a realist also aids in your contentment, which brings happiness, that, which should be the focused pinnacle of our lives.

Cancer Cure

Oh Sister of hope! You have done your plight,
Your soul flies high beyond the skies.
With an energy that mesmerizes;
The strength you've showed will be amortized.

Oh, sisters here, let's all persist,
On cancer cure we will insist.
To end the curse that spoils our dreams,
Our children's future is at risk.

Our loved ones died, we know not why,
Because we are still in denial.
With fortune we must persevere,
And fight against that cancerous snare.

Oh, sister dear, we love you so!
Your strength we know will help us grow,
And learn to search without resist,
For cancer cure and stop the blitz.

Beauty on the Bay

Oh! How beautiful is the gleam before my eyes,
As the waters move, a blessing to be alive.
I see such joy amidst the shimmering blues.
How glorious it is to hear the ocean's snooze.

How wonderful to feel the freshness of life.
With graceful peace, the waters groove along.
Like throngs of lakes, with little ones connect,
As kids in unity, they play and bounce upon the deck.

The tides, it all depends on nature's day.
As human moods, it sometimes changes its course.
And when we least expect, it comes our way,
In faith we know it will be calmed next day.

The rolling waves suggest that we can play.
As the surf flushes unto our feet, we'll stray.
It is so cool; what a joy to spend the day.
With this friend, it is a pleasure to be in its way.

It is a vision of beauty on the bay.
As nature takes its course, we will not cease to pray.
For peace and love among the tide of day.
Be still, my friend—he will say on that appointed day.

We Might As Well Dance

I closed my eyes and then I saw.
A star, it shines in the distance far.
I felt a joy within my soul.
The halo around was in perfect gold.

I danced for joy of the vision I beheld.
And looked to the sky as our future unfolded.
It was a message of love sent from above,
A circle of gold means everlasting love.

So keep on dancing as the joy unfolds.
You are chosen since the days of old.
I will guide you, go on!
The story will unfold.

They come from the north,
And they come from the south,
The east and west,
That's man's great quest.

Amazed, they asked
What it is all about.
They are all mine, listen!
That is what the sound is about.

The Journey Ends

I followed them, I knew not where,
In conscious spirit, we seemed aware,
The leaves were green; the skies were blue,
The message seemed as if it were true.

A narrow road with tracks and turns,
A path that slopes as it upturns,
A stream we meet to get refreshed,
Because the uphill is the next.

We crossed the stream—it was so clean,
The shadows we can see in between,
There came a joy that brought relief,
Our soul, it surely was not grieved.

There was a rock—it seemed intact,
With a stream on top; I was attract,
I tapped the rock while on the track,
My heart, it felt for just that rock.

The hill was steep—I could have wept,
The peak I fear, I could not meet,
I saw a pit; it was a scare,
The journey then became a smear.

The angel spread his wings to cheer,
As he believed that I was scared,
I held my faith and stepped right o'er,
The journey ended with adores.

The People Now

The people now
They are not sound,
I know something is really wrong,
They come from the east and from west,
And north and south, they are amongst the best.

The people now that is around,
A pound of flesh will make them sound,
So when you see them come around,
Remember, dear, to hold your ground.

The people now
Look in your eyes,
To see when it's time to disguise,
And when you think they are there to guide,
That's when you are mesmerized.

The people now
They may seem at rest,
But don't be fooled by their zest,
Because when you think you have the best,
That's when your life becomes a mess.

People of Humanity

We are well-intended people,
Made uniquely by his will,
In all color, creed, shape, size, and mind.
With freedom, he gave us life that we may shine.

He made us smart and to act through a heart.
With smiles, he watches his creation as an art.
So humble and patient, even with such powers in hand,
Like a rope, he allows us the full length so uniquely planned.

Even though in darkness he still holds our hand,
Before our birth, he already knows our plan.
As our thoughts and mind he so designed.
His linkage to us is the only one of its kind.

As we his children are placed on this his earth,
Artistically designed control by human's alert.
In addition, he grants us wisdom and love.
Our creativity and gift, they all came from above.

Thanks to the creator, in generosity we perceive.
We ask for forgiveness, but still we deceive.
Our test and our challenges to you we unreel.
We plea, oh Dear Father, please make us real.

We ask that you touch us in your dear own way,
And guide us to the light so we will not stray.
That your peace and love within our heart will stay.
Through humanity we'll exhibit your goodness each day.

Season

Although the poems appear to have been tailored on a particular season, the bigger picture is that our entire life comprises of many seasons not only related to the environment but also to common-sense, which, to a great extent, are linked to our physical condition. Therefore, we as individuals have choices as to how we approach these seasons, knowing that they come and they go. The success in going to a retreat is to set a goal and leaving without defeat.

Christmas: Years go, Years come

Years go, years come—Christmas!
A festive season turned havoc for some,
With focus on getting this and getting that,
Running here and there,
Buying this, that, and all that other crap,
All caught up in such bureaucratic trap.

Losing the real sentiment of the fact,
Labeling this and labeling that,
Such mystic glitters a makeup plot,
Love crazed all over the place,
Jumping around like a seasonal clown,
Crowding the malls all around town.

Parking-lot wars—no space to park,
Shoplifters' sites, what joy at last!
Purses and parcels, so much for snatching,
From Christmas celebs both far and near,
Money spenders swiping credit cards without care,
While Wall Street dealers muse in on the fund.

Drinking premium vodka, still whisky, and Wray rum.
While CEOs' bonus bucket leaks,
Of enormous payouts as the gravy train goes,
In the southern course, they gulf and blend,
As the underdogs struggle to exist on the lend,
With pressure so stressed as the New Year comes.

Credit cards to pay and no job around,
A corporate mess in this downsizing town,
Mutual funds, an offshore investment clash,
But in betrayal, attrition they proclaim,
With hiking bills—medical, utility, and taxes—it's a shame,
With such limited reserve, who knows what's next?

While conglomerates reap the benefits of you,
And on minimum wage you struggle through,
Already deflated before the rollout,
But Christmas is Christmas, so let there be fun,
Temporary but joyous, as an illusion flung,
Promises joy to the world all year round.

Abundant love for one and all,
For you and for me, so let's all be true,
With the spirit of support, of unity, and of love,
To fight against the selfish snub,
The corporate system, an industrial ploy,
Religious wisdom is a must to be deployed.

With vital reasoning, you will be amazed,
On this special season of peace and of love,
Of jingling songs so delightfully sweet,
As the drummer boys beat in harmony, they meet,
What joy it is to be at such a retreat,
So with wisdom in unity, let's make merry without defeat!

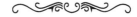

So . . . It Is Christmas

This is the period for giving, of love and cheers,
To wipe away all tears and overcome all fears,
To bring the spirit of joy in this world's affairs,
The season to be jolly and bursting in cares.

Of sugar and spice and all that's nice,
Sparkles and glitters, green, red, oh so bright,
Of parties with candy, of liquors that spike,
A world so filled with great delights.

Of laughter and dancing and caroling all night,
This'd be Christmas—it's for sharing,
No curse, no swearing nor fights,
Applauding, best wishes for a special season so bright.

Of parties celebrating the birth of a child,
And concerts in replay of the Nativity sight,
While echoes of sweet music in the distance it glides,
And for nine mornings, it's like a rainbow in the skies.

Eight days, seven days, six days, we lime,
Five, four, three, we count down the chimes,
Two is the eve when rum cake we smell,
Then arriving on Christmas morning is Santa, all
jolly and swell!

The Lampstand

It's the season to be jolly,
It's the season to be bright,
Just the memories are the reason,
For all the fuss, the cheers and lights.

But for some, it is just a season,
Of a lampstand within their sights,
In a world so filled with darkness,
Blinded by such, its elusive plights.

As the lampstand stood there burning,
For a child so full of glow,
So full of light and promise of hope,
A child with peace for one and all.

Through him today we see the glory,
Then to some he was just a child,
Today we know he is that lampstand,
Our miracle and strength day after day.

That light that shines above the cross,
Adorned with bows and seasonal twigs,
Sprinkled so gracefully with snow or rain,
How tranquil such blessing that heals the pain.

So as we see that lampstand's light,
Let us not forget the unfortunate,
As this season is for the sharing of delight,
To those so loved and those with plight.

And as the lonely lampstands gleam,
A seasonal reminder, the need to share your joys,
So look around and take a stand,
Lighting the lampstands of those unfortunate ones!

A Special Christmas and Prosperous New Year

Christmas, a special time for giving,
Of love and cheers, to wipe away all tears,
Bringing the spirit of joy in this world's affairs,
A season to be jolly and bursting with cares.

Of sugar and spice and all that's nice,
Sparkles, glitters, green, red, a world so bright,
Of parties with candy, of liquors and appetites,
In a world so filled with great delights.

Of laughter and dancing and caroling all night,
This'd be Christmas—it's for sharing,
No curse, no swearing, nor squabble or fights,
Just cheers and thrills from the spirit of delight.

To shop and shop around the clock,
There're gifts, more gifts—where do we stop?
The time to spend, it is the trend,
While the New Year creeps around the bend.

So as we move beyond the season's twirl,
And the New Year comes for one and all,
As rainbows of fireworks adorn the skies,
And champagne spouts amid the crowds.

Let's wish for peace, let's wish for love,
And all good blessings from heaven above,
For unity and honor, sincerity we foster,
As we the people move forward to prosper.

Edwards Brothers Malloy
Oxnard, CA USA
October 9, 2014